THE
HEADLESS
TEACHER

THE FANG GANG

THE HEADLESS TEACHER

Roy Apps

Illustrated by

Sumiko Shimakata

BLOOMSBURY

To Tom – R.A.

To AKY – S.S.

Published in Great Britain in 2006 by Bloomsbury Publishing Plc,
36 Soho Square, London, W1D 3QY

A CIP catalogue record of this book is available from the British Library

ISBN 978 07475 8359 2

Printed in Great Britain by Clays Ltd, St Ives Plc

3 5 7 9 10 8 6 4

All papers used by Bloomsbury Publishing are natural,
recyclable products made from wood grown in well-managed forests.
The manufacturing processes conform to the environmental
regulations of the country of origin.

Chapter 1

THE DAY THE BRAZILIAN rainforest went up in flames I was looking at a note that Tiffany had left me under my English draft book.

The fire had started innocently enough; just a wispy column of smoke. Then, all of a sudden, flames leapt upwards towards the ceiling.

Gory, who had been holding a magnifying glass over the 'Brazil' page of the class atlas, right in the path of a strong shaft of sunlight, started shouting: 'Fire! Fire!' Everybody else in the class began screaming and running about.

'Sit down, everyone!' ordered Mr Cheng, our teacher, grabbing a bottle of water from the lunch-box rack and pouring it over the flames.

Nobody took any notice of Mr Cheng. Instead, we all stood around looking at the

charred remains of the atlas and getting very excited.

'Sit down!' yelled Mr Cheng again.

Mr Cheng was new. He would have struggled to keep a row of pencils in order, let alone a class of thirty pupils at Goolish School; a class which included a werewolf, a ghoul and two vampires.

'Who is responsible for this?' asked Mr Cheng, crossly. Everyone knew it was Gory, but nobody said anything. We just looked blank.

I took another peek at Tiffany's note:

Dear Jonathan

First meeting of the 'Stake and Garlic Club'. Morning break. By the bins in the playground. Be there!

Tiffany xx Vampire Slayer

p.s. You shall be my second in command (unless someone better turns up).

I could have ignored Tiffany's note of course. But what would have been the point? She would only have come looking for me and our school playground is no place for a hunted man. There is nowhere to hide.

Mr Cheng let us go out for break almost before the bell had rung. I don't think he could stand being in our class a minute longer. I made my way out to the playground to meet Tiffany. When I got to the bins, she was already there.

'The Stake and Garlic Club. It's a great name, isn't it?' she said, tossing her head in the air. 'But then I've always been clever with words. Stakes and garlic: the two things that strike fear into the heart of every vampire. And that's what this club is all about.'

'Where are the rest of the members?' I asked.

Tiffany sighed. 'I invited loads of people, but nobody else seems to have turned up. They're just too stupid and lazy. Looks like it's just you and me, Jonathan. We've got to stop them. Scarlet and her friends, and that disgusting old

man at the traffic lights!' She meant my grandad. 'You saw him! His image didn't come out on the camera! And another thing. I saw him again on Saturday. He was in a coffin on top of a hearse, waving his arms about. And in the hearse were Scarlet, Griselda and Gory. Can you believe it?'

Believe it? Of course I could believe it. I'd been there. Hiding under the front seat. Not that Tiffany knew that, otherwise I would hardly have been attending the first meeting of her Stake and Garlic Club, would I?

'They've got to be stopped,' Tiffany said, grinding her teeth.

'Why?' I asked, innocently.

'Why?' said Tiffany, outraged. 'Because . . . because they are not nice people for a start.' She came up close and whispered to me in a disgusted tone of voice, 'Don't you see? They're *different!*'

What I *could* see, out of the corner of my eye, was Scarlet looking in my direction. Her expression was anything but friendly. Suddenly, Tiffany turned and waved to Mr Cheng. He was on playground duty. Just his luck.

'Oh, isn't he lush?' simpered Tiffany. Mr Cheng was her favourite teacher. She sat at her desk making puppy-dog eyes at him all day. She ran across to him. I followed. To tell you the truth, I felt a bit sorry for the guy, having to teach a class like ours all day.

'Hello, Tiffany. Hello, Jonathan,' said Mr Cheng, nervously.

'Mr Cheng,' whispered Tiffany, with a snivelling

sort of whine in her voice, 'I know who set the Brazilian rainforest alight. It was Gory. I saw him.'

'Oh?' said Mr Cheng. And you could tell he didn't like snitches any more than the rest of us.

'Yes,' Tiffany went on. 'And I can't say I'm surprised. He hangs around with the Fang Gang.'

'The Fang Gang?' Mr Cheng repeated with a frown. 'Who are the Fang Gang?'

'They are,' said Tiffany, pointing towards the far side of the playground, where Scarlet, Griselda and Gory were skulking looking suitably toothsome and gruesome. 'They reckon they're from the dark side. You know, werewolves and vampires.'

'Really?' said Mr Cheng. 'Tell me more.'

But at that moment there was a blood-curdling scream from the direction of the picnic tables and Mr Cheng had to amble off to try and sort out a fight.

'So, Jonathan,' said Tiffany menacingly, when

he had gone, 'it's just over three weeks until the next full moon. That's three weeks the Stake and Garlic Club – that's you and me – have got to plan how to slay every vampire in Goolish.'

In a way, I was relieved. It meant that Tiffany Bliss (Vampire Slayer) still had no idea that I, Jonathan Leech, was a vampire.

And I hoped it would stay that way. For a very long time.

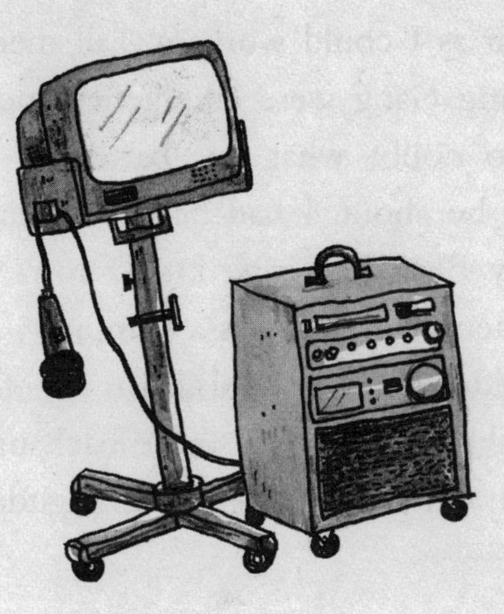

Chapter 2

WHEN I GOT BACK to the classroom I found another note under my English draft book.

Jonathan
There will be an emergency meeting of the Fang Gang tonight at dusk in the old hut on the far side of the graveyard.
Be there! Scarlet

As far as I could work out, all meetings of the Fang Gang were emergency meetings. I had no doubt what this particular meeting would be about. I had been seen talking to Tiffany Bliss. The gang knew, from what I'd told them, that she was a vampire slayer and they didn't want to be slayed.

Quickly, I slipped the note back under my English draft book as Mr Cheng glided by.

Mr Cheng didn't have much luck keeping order after break. It was Friday and just about everybody was restless. Only Tiffany was hanging on Mr Cheng's every word which was: 'Quiet! Will you please get on with your work!' To the rest of the class, he might just as well have been invisible.

I spent all lunchtime avoiding Tiffany. I didn't want the Fang Gang to get any more wrong ideas. I avoided the Fang Gang too; I didn't want Tiffany getting any *right* ideas.

What a mess! If I didn't join Tiffany's Stake and Garlic Club, she'd get all suspicious and carry on with her plans to slay every vampire, ghoul, zombie and werewolf in Goolish anyway. If I *did* join Tiffany's Stake and Garlic Club, the Fang Gang would accuse me of being a traitor.

It was a lose-lose situation, I thought glumly as, after lunch, I trudged out on to the school field for football practice. I'd never been much good at football in the past, but I'd found out that because of my growing vampire skill of power running, I was actually now rather good at it.

In fact, Mr Hacker, our PE teacher, said, 'Jonathan, you're a proper little dynamo. I definitely want you in the team to play against Lady Daphne Freebody's in the Inter-Schools' Cup match.'

Jonathan Leech, football star. Cool! *Perhaps I should I call myself* Jonno *Leech*, I thought, as I pushed open the broken gate to Drac's Cottage, my grandad's place. Suddenly, a dreadful noise filled my ears.

'Bee Boppa Loola. She's ma bay-beeee! Yee-eh!'

A flock of startled rooks wheeled above the woods behind the cottage, squawking in terror.

I dashed inside. There in the kitchen stood Grandad, a terrifying smile playing across his toothless mouth. In his hand he held a microphone, which was connected to a battered karaoke machine.

'Ah, Jonathan, boy! What do you reckon, eh?'

Bottles of blood rattled on the shelves of the Welsh dresser.

'Turn it off, Grandad!' I ordered.

Grandad switched off the karaoke machine. 'I got it from Mort the undertaker,' he explained. 'He used to use it up at the graveyard when the ghosts and the undead wanted to party. Do you know they have their own

talent show up there called *The X-toplasm Factor*?'

'Grandad, what on earth do you need a karaoke machine for?' I asked.

Grandad looked put out. 'Can't an old man try and bring a little sunshine into his life?' he muttered.

'I didn't think you liked sunshine,' I reminded him. 'I thought you preferred lying in your coffin in a darkened room.'

'But if the sunshine is on the face of a beautiful woman, that's different,' replied Grandad, with a kind of wicked twinkle in his eye.

An appalling thought struck me. 'Grandad! You're not in love?'

Grandad shrugged. 'You have a problem with that?'

'Too right I have!' I said.

'Because I'm a vampire?'

'No,' I replied, 'because you're *old*!'

Grandad switched off the karaoke machine with a moody shrug. 'Your tea's already on the table,' he said. 'I'm going upstairs for a quiet lie-down in my coffin.'

There was a postcard on my plate. I picked it up. It was from my dad.

SS *Albatross,* South Atlantic Ocean

Just had a card from your gran to say she's in prison and you are in Goolish! As soon as I can, I will find a way out of there for you. In the meantime, DON'T TOUCH THE KETCHUP!

Your loving dad

PS: DON'T TOUCH THE SAUSAGES EITHER!

Jonathan Leech
c/o Mr Leech
Drac's Cottage
Goolish

It was very good of Dad to say he'd find a way out of Goolish for me. I wasn't going to hold my breath though. He meant well, but my dad was one of those people who struggled to find their way out of the multi-storey car park. He'd never find a way of getting me out of Goolish. No, I was here until my mum and dad came back from their Antarctic cruise or my gran got out of prison, where she was being held for supermarket-trolley-rage offences.

Tea was sausages. I ignored Dad's advice and tucked in. Grandad's sausages were made from a special vampire recipe and were delicious. I suddenly felt bad for moaning about his karaoke machine. It was just that I *knew* he was up to something. And although I'd not been staying with him for long, I'd already learnt that when Grandad was up to something, it always spelt trouble.

Whatever Grandad put in his sausages must have been some sort of brain food. Because although I spent half an hour after tea failing to work out any of the answers to my last week's maths homework, I *did* manage to work out a solution to the Tiffany Bliss problem!

A solution to the Tiffany Bliss problem *and* a future career as a football star. As the night drew in and I set off to the meeting of the Fang Gang, I was feeling rather pleased with myself.

Chapter 3

THE FANG GANG'S headquarters was half hidden under an enormous yew tree. The door was unlocked and I went straight in. The rest of the gang – Scarlet, Gory, Griselda and Crombie the Zombie – were already there. So was Little Alfie, who Griselda had to babysit for. Hc was a mummy's boy in more ways than one. They all looked at me but not a word of greeting was spoken.

Scarlet cleared her throat. 'I declare this emergency meeting of the Fang Gang open,' she announced. 'Item one: this.'

Scarlet took a piece of paper from her pocket and held it up for everyone to see. 'I found this on the floor of the classroom. It's an invitation to the first meeting of something called the 'Stake and Garlic Club'. Signed by Tiffany Bliss. The meeting was held at lunchtime today by the bins in the playground. Only one person was seen with Tiffany Bliss in the playground at lunchtime.' Scarlet looked hard at me. 'You, Jonathan. Do you confess to having attended the first meeting of the Stake and Garlic Club?'

'Yes,' I said.

'Go on! Admit it!' yelled Gory, stabbing a finger in my direction. 'Lying won't help you! We have proof!'

'Gory,' said Griselda, 'sit down.'

'I'll force a confession from him, even if I have to tear him apart with my bare hands!' roared Gory.

'Gory, he's admitted it! Now be quiet!' ordered Scarlet.

Gory stood there, a look of puzzled disappointment on his face. 'Has he? Oh. Typical.'

'In fact,' I went on, 'unless there has been a sudden surge in membership since dinner time, I'm fifty per cent of the members of the Stake and Garlic Club.'

'Wow,' said Crombie the Zombie. 'Is that cool? Or is that cool?'

'And judging by its name,' Scarlet continued, 'I don't suppose the aim of the Stake and Garlic Club is to be particularly nice and friendly to members of the Fang Gang.'

'No,' I agreed. 'In fact, the aim of the Stake and Garlic Club is to slay every vampire, ghoul, werewolf and zombie in Goolish on the night of the next full moon.'

'I don't want to be slayed,' wailed Little Alfie. 'I want my mummy!'

'Now look what you've done,' said Scarlet, crossly.

'It's all right, Alfie,' soothed Griselda, 'nobody is going to be slayed.'

Little Alfie stopped sobbing, which was a relief. Nobody – apart from Little Alfie himself, of course – wanted his mummy charging into the hut, throwing her weight and her bandages about.

'You wanted to know what the aims of the Stake and Garlic Club were,' I retorted, crossly.

'The point is, Jonathan,' said Scarlet, 'you're a self-confessed member of Tiffany's Stake and Garlic Club, but you're also a vampire. Just what are you playing at?'

'It's simple,' I explained. 'If I hadn't turned up for the Stake and Garlic Club at dinner time, Tiffany would have been really suspicious. But you see the advantages of me being on your side?'

The way Scarlet and the others all sat around frowning at me, it was obvious that they didn't. And why should they? They hadn't had the benefit of a double helping of Grandad's sausages for tea. I explained my plan.

'If I'm in the Stake and Garlic Club, I can report to the Fang Gang on the sort of things Tiffany is planning, and I can feed her duff information about the Gang and the dark side.'

'We'll always be one step ahead of her game!' exclaimed Scarlet.

'He'll be like a double agent!' added Griselda, excitedly.

'Cool,' said Crombie the Zombie.

Only Gory didn't look convinced. 'How do we know he's telling the truth?' he asked. 'He *says* he'll be a double agent. How do we know he'll not become a *triple* agent?'

'Or a quadruple agent?' suggested Crombie. 'Or a *quin*tuple agent –'

'Crombie, shut up,' said Griselda.

'I believe him. Now he's explained himself,' said Scarlet. 'It all makes sense.'

'I'm not convinced,' said Gory.

'Oh, nothing would ever convince you of anything,' replied Griselda, grumpily.

'How do we *know* he's one of us?' said Gory. 'Just because he can put on a turn of speed. I mean, if you're from the dark side you've got to be well scary. But look at him. Scary? I've seen scarier-looking jelly babies.'

The Fang Gang all turned to look at me. And their looks said: yeh, maybe Gory *has* got a point.

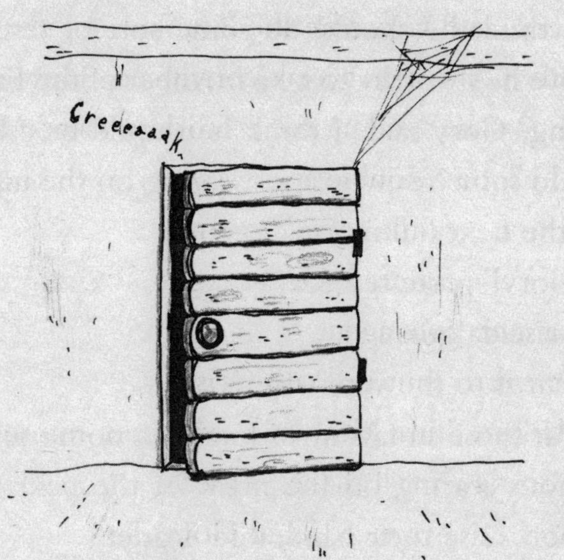

Chapter 4

THE TRUTH WAS, Gory had always been suspicious of me. And the fact that my newly developed power-running skills had suddenly made me – rather than him – the star of the school football team hadn't done anything to endear me to him, either. In fact, with me in the team, there was some doubt as to whether or not Gory would be playing at all in the Inter-Schools' Cup match. No wonder he was sore.

'I think he should do some sort of test to prove he's worthy to be a member of the Fang Gang,' Gory said. 'I think he should be asked to do some really serious scaring on the night of the next full moon.'

'Gory!' protested Scarlet.

Griselda groaned.

'Put it to the vote,' said Gory.

'All those in favour of Jonathan doing some serious scaring on the night of the next full moon, raise their hand,' said Scarlet.

Scarlet and Griselda kept their hands down. So did Little Alfie, who wasn't old enough to vote, anyway. Gory and Crombie put their hands up. Then I put my hand up. I suppose it was a daft thing to do really, but I didn't want to look a wimp in front of the others.

'Huh, boys!' said Griselda with disgust.

'This meeting of the Fang Gang resolves that Jonathan should do some serious scaring on the night of the next full moon,' said Scarlet with a sigh. 'All those in favour of the suggestion that Jonathan should continue his involvement with the Stake and Garlic Club so that he can act as a double agent?'

Everyone put up their hands.

'Meeting closed,' said Scarlet.

There was a moment's silence. A silence that was suddenly broken by the sound of a slow, sinister hammering on the door.

'I want my mum . . .' began Little Alfie, before Griselda clamped a hand over his dribbling mouth.

We all looked at each other.

'I don't like it,' whispered Gory, shaking like a leaf.

'You're a ghoul, for goodness' sake,' hissed Griselda. 'How can you be scared of noises in a graveyard?'

Scarlet looked long and hard at me. 'You

don't think it's Tiffany, do you? You don't think she's sussed your plan of becoming a double agent?'

I remembered a strange feeling I'd had of being followed and a shadow I thought I'd seen disappearing behind a gravestone. I gulped. But before I could speak, the door began to open.

We all shrank back into the far corner of the hut. The door stayed half open but nobody appeared. Then a voice spoke:

'Would it be all right if I came in?'

It was a voice that Griselda, Scarlet, Gory and I recognised immediately. Not Tiffany, but—

'Mr Cheng?' asked Scarlet, incredulously.

'Yes, it's me,' said Mr Cheng. 'I'd like to come into your hut, but I should warn you it might be a bit of a shock.'

'You haven't brought us extra maths homework, have you?' asked Griselda, in a suspicious tone.

'No, I haven't!' insisted Mr Cheng.

'Then, er . . . of course, Mr Cheng, you'd better come in,' said Scarlet.

And into the hut came Mr Cheng. Well, to be precise, into the hut came Mr Cheng's feet, legs, body and arms. What didn't come into the hut was Mr Cheng's head. It appeared to be missing.

'Aaargh!' said Gory, Griselda, Scarlet and I.

'I want my m-m-m-m . . .' yelled Little Alfie, before Griselda could get her hand to his mouth, again.

'Hey, man, way cool,' said Crombie.

Chapter 5

IF YOU'VE EVER MET a headless teacher you will know that the whole thing can be a bit of a shock. Particularly if, like Mr Cheng, it's a *talking* headless teacher. I mean, you never quite know when they're going to say something because you can't see their lips move.

'Er . . . I did say it might be a bit of a shock,' said Mr Cheng suddenly and we all jumped.

'Where's your head?' asked Scarlet. Which in the circumstances, I suppose, was the only sensible question to ask.

'I was rather hoping you'd be able to tell me that,' said Mr Cheng, sadly.

'He says he's Mr Cheng, but how do we *know* he's Mr Cheng?' whispered Gory. He had a point. How do you tell if someone is who they say they are if you can't see their face?

'Of course it's Mr Cheng,' said Scarlet. 'Don't you recognise his voice?'

'And the scorch marks on his cuffs where he put out the flaming atlas this morning,' added Griselda.

Well, that was proof enough for me. Gory nodded too. And then, of course, we all had about a million questions to ask Mr Cheng. Unfortunately, we asked them all at once. Mr Cheng put his hands over his ears – or rather he put his hands over where his ears would have been if he'd had a head.

'I think I'd better start at the beginning,' said Mr Cheng. 'So, listen carefully. I'll be setting you a test afterwards.'

'What!' exclaimed Gory.

'Only joking,' said Mr Cheng.

Gory didn't look totally convinced.

'I'm a vampire,' said Mr Cheng, 'descended from a long line of Chinese vampires. In China, all vampires have the ability to remove their heads.'

'Is that why you got a job at Goolish

School? Because you're a vampire?' asked Griselda.

Mr Cheng nodded. 'I wanted to work in a school where some of the pupils would be from the dark side. Ms Blossom, your delightful head teacher, told me some of her pupils were young vampires, ghouls and werewolves, though for the life of her she could never remember which. It wasn't until Tiffany mentioned the Fang Gang to me that I worked it out.'

'How did you know we'd be here?' asked Scarlet.

'A glance at the note you slipped under Jonathan's English draft book was enough to tell me that,' said Mr Cheng. 'And now, I very much need your help.'

'Why, what's the problem, man?' asked Crombie.

'Oh, for goodness' sake, Crombie,' snapped Griselda. 'Mr Cheng's lost his head.'

Crombie shrugged. 'So? Miss Goonhilly, our class teacher, has lost her brains, but nobody suggests we should help her find them.'

Griselda groaned. 'I'm sorry, Mr Cheng, you'll have to excuse Crombie, he's a –'

'Zombie. Yes, I gathered as much,' said Mr Cheng. And if he'd had his head on him I'm sure he would have nodded it.

'Where exactly did you lose your head, Mr Cheng?' asked Scarlet.

'It was after school,' said Mr Cheng. 'I'd had a lousy afternoon, what with the class mucking about . . .' Here, Gory, Griselda, Scarlet and I all felt Mr Cheng's eyes piercing us severely, even though, of course, he hadn't got any. It was weird. 'But of course,' Mr Cheng went on, sharply, 'you lot know all about that.'

We nodded.

'I went to the staffroom, which was empty, took off my head and put it on the table to give it a rest. Suddenly, I heard someone coming. I dived into the staff toilets, leaving my head on the table in my panic. I heard this person come and go. Just as I was about to go back into the staffroom, I heard someone else coming. I dived back into the toilets. Next, I heard the toilet door being locked and all the lights went out. It had been the caretaker coming round to lock up the school! I waited till it got dark then managed to get out through the toilet window.

'And then you came up here?' asked Scarlet.

Mr Cheng nodded. 'You see, the thing is, I can't go banging on the door of the caretaker's

house to say: "Can you let me into school, only I've left my head in the staffroom", can I? But then I thought, what about the Fang Gang? They might have the power to shimmer through walls, turn into bats, use superhuman strength . . . Perhaps they could break into school and get my head back! Well, what about it?'

'Can't you get your own head back?' said Gory, grumpily. 'You're a vampire. Haven't you got superhuman strength?'

'No, I haven't,' said Mr Cheng. 'The only gift that Chinese vampires have is the gift of being able to remove their heads.'

'Huh, useless,' muttered Gory.

'On the contrary, it's a very useful gift indeed,' said Mr Cheng, crossly. 'For example, if you want a haircut, you can just leave your head at the hairdresser's for half an hour or so. No need to waste time sitting around reading celebrity magazines or listening to the hairdresser twitter on about last night's TV programmes.'

'Of course we can get your head back, Mr Cheng!' said Griselda. 'We'll meet say . . . nine o'clock tomorrow outside the school?'

We all agreed to that.

'If it's all the same with you,' Mr Cheng said, 'I'll lie low in my bedsit. I think a headless teacher hanging about the school gates might look a little bit suspicious. I'll meet you here after dark and you can give me my head back,' said Mr Cheng.

'Yeh, no problem, man,' said Crombie.

But that was where Crombie was wrong. Very wrong indeed.

Chapter 6

NEXT MORNING, Grandad cooked liver and black pudding for breakfast. After that I went straight out and walked down the hill into town, ready to meet the rest of the Fang Gang at the school gates.

I was coming round the corner by Veronica Vickers' knicker shop when I saw Tiffany and her mum. Short of actually diving into the knicker shop, there was no way of avoiding them.

'Jonathan!' Tiffany called. 'Fancy seeing you here! It must be fate.'

'Must it?' I asked.

'Hello, Jonathan!' cooed Mrs Bliss. She turned to Tiffany. 'Now, I'm sure you and Jonathan have things to chat about.'

'No, we don't,' I said. But Mrs Bliss ignored me.

'Come and find me in Veronica Vickers' when you're done,' she said to Tiffany. And she disappeared into the shop.

'Right, Jonathan,' said Tiffany. 'You and I have some shopping to do.'

She made it sound as if we'd got to go off to buy the week's groceries.

'Sorry, busy!' I said, hurrying off.

Tiffany was not one of those girls who take no for an answer, still less one of those girls who take 'Sorry, busy' for an excuse. She started running after me.

'Jonathan, wait!'

I stopped and waited for her. Short of having her follow me to the school gates, there was nothing else I could do.

'The Stake and Garlic Club,' said Tiffany. 'Haven't you realised there's something missing?'

Like members? I thought, but I didn't say it.

'We don't have any stakes!' declared Tiffany.

'Don't have any garlic, either,' I pointed out.

'Garlic my mum always has. In a funny little pot on the window sill,' said Tiffany. 'But stakes she hasn't got. Which is why you and I are going to buy some.'

'Now?' I thought of the trouble I'd be in if I was late for the Fang Gang.

'Why not now? The way I see it, there's no time to lose. Full moon is less than three weeks away. And we'll need to practise so that we get it right on the night.'

I tried to imagine how you *practise* hammering a stake through someone's heart, but pretty soon gave up.

Tiffany steered me into the DIY shop.

'Have you got any stakes?' she asked the shop assistant, who jerked a thumb towards the yard at the back of the store.

There were lots of stakes. All of them about three and a half metres long. They were ideal material for rose arches and the like, but not so hot for vampire slaying. Not that I was about to tell Tiffany that.

'They're just right,' said Tiffany, her face set hard. 'We'll need them long if we're going to do the job properly.' She went over to the shop assistant. 'Twelve of those stakes, please,' she said.

'Twelve?' I gasped.

'Well, we'll need more eventually, of course. I reckon, if we're to slay every vampire in Goolish, twelve will be enough to be getting on with.'

Tiffany took a wad of notes from her shoulder bag and handed them to the shop assistant. Then she gave her address and fixed a delivery date. Just like that.

'Have you done this sort of thing before?' I asked her.

'Vampire slaying? No. Shopping? Yes,' replied Tiffany.

Outside the shop Tiffany said, 'The stakes are arriving at my place on Monday. We'd better have a Stake and Garlic Club meeting after school.'

We stood outside 'Veronica Vickers: Beautiful Knickers'.

'Er, I really ought to go,' I said, desperately.

'Yes, I think you ought,' said Tiffany. Not even she was daft enough to want to be seen with a boy in 'Veronica Vickers: Beautiful Knickers'.

Chapter 7

As Tiffany disappeared into the shop, I ran as fast as I could to the gates of Goolish School.

To my amazement, the rest of the gang were all standing about outside the gates. They looked utterly fed up. Little Alfie was with them. Perhaps that was why.

'You're late,' moaned Scarlet.

'You could've started without me,' I replied.

Griselda, Scarlet, Crombie and Little Alfie all turned to look at Gory, who looked embarrassed.

'There's a padlock on the door as well as a Yale,' said Griselda. 'Gory shimmered through but couldn't open it from the other side.'

'So, we want you to use your vampire strength to break the lock in two,' said Scarlet, brightly.

'Right,' I said, with a gulp.

'Huh,' snorted Gory.

Checking that no one was watching, we made our way across the playground to the school door. I grasped the lock and squeezed. Nothing happened. Out of the corner of my eye, I saw Gory sniggering. That really riled me. I shut my eyes tight and I thought vampire thoughts. Slowly, the metal in my hands seemed to warm up and started to feel not like metal, but clay. I squeezed some more and heard the sound of a clunk at my feet. I looked down and saw the broken pieces of metal that had been the padlock.

Gory and Griselda stared, open-mouthed. Little Alfie clapped his hands and Scarlet grinned at me.

'Hey man, way cool,' said Crombie.

Griselda turned the handle on the door. It opened and in we went. We made our way down the corridor to the staffroom. Inside the staffroom there was a huge table. On it were old newspapers, punctured footballs, taped-up hockey sticks, broken maracas and a half-eaten banana and coleslaw sandwich, but no head. We all stared at each other in horror.

'Now let's think about this carefully, guys,' said Griselda, a touch of panic in her voice. 'Who would want to take Mr Cheng's head from the staffroom and why?'

'Mr Cheng said the caretaker came in and locked up. Perhaps he cleared up too?' suggested Scarlet.

'But, if he cleared up, why did he leave the table in such a disgusting state?' asked Gory.

'Caretakers don't clean tables. They just clean floors,' said Crombie.

'Perhaps Mr Cheng's head rolled on to the floor!' I said.

'In which case the caretaker would've taken it to the lost-property cupboard!' declared Griselda. 'Come on!'

We ran back along the corridor to the lost-property cupboard. The stink in there was overwhelming. No wonder, because it was chock-full of old socks and moth-eaten trainers. There was also a Man U shirt with one arm missing, an Action Man and a stuffed parrot. But there was no head.

'Look, it's Polly the Parrot!' everyone exclaimed, except me.

'Excuse me, but how can you *lose* a stuffed parrot?' I asked.

'Simple,' explained Griselda. 'It belonged to this kid called Kyle, who brought it into

school for our pirate play. Scarlet did her vanishing trick, crept up behind the parrot and said in a parrot voice, "I'm going to pluck out your eyes for my supper tonight." Kyle ran off screaming and refused to take the parrot home.'

'Want Polly!' yelled Little Alfie.

'You can't have Polly,' snapped Griselda.

'Want Polly!' yelled Little Alfie again. At least it made a change from his usual 'I want my mummy' yell.

'It's no good,' I shouted above Little Alfie's din. 'We're never going to find Mr Cheng's head at this rate. I mean, it could be anywhere.'

'What are we going to do? Mr Cheng can't come to school on Monday without a head,' said Scarlet.

'He might have a better chance of keeping the class in order if he did,' muttered Gory.

'There's only one thing for it,' I said. 'We'll just have to make him a false one.'

'We can't do that!' replied Griselda, aghast.

'Why not?' I asked. 'We're in school. We've got all the stuff we need here, in the art room. Paint, glue . . .'

'Wannapaint!' screamed Little Alfie.

That clinched it. Off to the art room we went.

Chapter 8

I DON'T KNOW IF you've made many false heads, but believe me, it is not as easy as it looks. For a start, with somebody like Mr Cheng, who although he was missing a real head still had a 'virtual' one on top of his neck, it was no good making something solid. I drew a diagram for the others to show what I meant:

False head ...
'Virtual' head
Hello
Neck
Body
Feet

We ended up making something rather like a big helmet for Mr Cheng to slip over his 'virtual' head. Griselda was a dab hand with the PVA glue and we found a mop to use for hair. We couldn't find any brushes, but when you've got somebody like Scarlet with the hands of a werewolf in your gang that sort of thing doesn't really become a problem. Little Alfie fell asleep in the brown paint, so we had to give Mr Cheng's false head purple eyebrows instead. Still, that couldn't be helped.

It was then that we heard a voice down the corridor.

'Hello? Who's there?'

'It's the caretaker,' hissed Griselda. 'Quick! The fire doors.'

Scarlet shoved the head into a black sack and we dashed across the art room to the fire doors, knocking over pots of paint, glue and water as we went. Then we remembered Little Alfie was still asleep in the brown paint, so we had to go back for him, knocking over more paint, glue and water as we did so.

Once outside, we dashed across the playground and straight out of the school gates, Crombie and I carrying the half-sleeping Little Alfie.

When we reached the sea front, we reckoned we were out of danger.

'There's nothing more we can do now until we meet Mr Cheng this evening,' said Griselda. 'Scarlet, you take charge of the head. I'll come back with you. I'll have to get Little Alfie's faced scrubbed clean before I take him home.'

I made my way up the hill to Drac's Cottage and had reached Mort the undertaker's place when the faint sound of Grandad and his karaoke came wafting through the air.

Mort was polishing his hearse.

'Morning, Jonathan,' called Mort gloomily. 'Enjoying the weekend? Shame about the weather being so warm and sunny.'

'I think I'd enjoy the weekend even more if you'd only take your karaoke machine back from Grandad,' I said.

Mort shook his head. 'I can't do that,' he replied. 'I swapped him my karaoke machine for his old freezer. And you can't go back on a swap.'

'He says he's in love,' I sighed. 'I wish I knew who with.'

Mort shrugged. 'Who's to tell? It could be anybody, what with your grandad being such a ladies' man.'

It didn't make a lot of sense to me. I wondered, too, what Mort wanted with Grandad's old freezer. Then as I turned to make my way back up the hill towards Drac's Cottage, the sign above Mort's door caught my eye:

MORT'S MOTORS
MINIBUSES
Body Repair Workshop

I suppose a man like Mort had to keep his bodies somewhere.

Chapter 9

AS I WALKED INTO the kitchen of Drac's Cottage, the sound of Grandad's song filled my ears.

'I'm a big, bad, scary vampire
And I'm in love, by heck,
So why not let me take a bite
From your lovely, slender neck? Oh yeh . . .?'

At least Grandad had the decency to stop as soon as he saw me standing there. He had a sort of sheepish smile on his face. I thought of what Mort had said about him being a 'ladies' man' and shivered. Whatever Grandad was planning, I just knew it would mean trouble.

'There's a postcard come for you, boy,' Grandad announced.

It was from Dad:

SS *Albatross,* South Atlantic Ocean

Dear Jonathan
We saw our first penguin the day before yesterday. We saw about two thousand more yesterday and about another three thousand today. It's difficult to be absolutely precise about the figure as they all look the same. Brilliant news! I've met a retired SAS officer on board. It won't be long now! Keep smiling! Mum sends her love.
Love Dad

Jonathan Leech
c/o Mr Leech
Drac's Cottage
Goolish

Grandad looked at me, sadly. 'Penguins? Retired SAS officers? I'm afraid your dad has gone quite off his head,' he said. 'It sometimes happens to people who are forced to spend long periods at sea.'

'I suppose he is terrified of me turning into a vampire,' I said.

Grandad nodded. 'To tell you the truth, it was a great disappointment to me when I realised that your dad wasn't going to grow up into a vampire. But then, the gift often skips a generation.'

'When did you know that he wasn't going to become a vampire?' I asked.

'When he started going out with your mother,' replied Grandad, 'instead of getting himself a nice ghoul-friend like the other lads his age.'

'I've got to do some serious scaring at next full moon, to prove to Gory that I'm a proper vampire,' I said. 'And I'm really worried I won't be able to manage it.'

Grandad nodded. 'You can't really call yourself a vampire if you can't scare people.'

'Really? I can power run and I'm developing superhuman strength,' I said.

Grandad snorted. 'Superhuman strength, power runs, turning into a bat . . . they're all very handy things in themselves, but scaring other folks senseless is what vampiring is really all about. No, you can't call yourself a vampire if you can't scare folks witless.'

'Do you think I could scare folks witless?' I asked, doubtfully.

Grandad looked hard at me, sighed and shook

his head. 'It would help if you at least *looked* scary,' he said. 'But you look positively *angelic*, boy, even on the spookiest of nights.' He put a hand on my shoulder. 'Don't worry, I'll try and think of something to make you scary.'

To be honest, he didn't sound too hopeful. As soon as he shuffled out of the kitchen and upstairs, I looked around for something to see my face in. There were no mirrors in Drac's Cottage, of course. Grandad had no need of them because, being a fully developed vampire, he had no reflection. I opened a drawer in the dresser and took out the biggest soup spoon I could find. I went up to my room, sat on my bed and peered into it. My face shone brightly back at me. Gory and Grandad were right. It was the least scary face in the whole of the solar system.

I turned to Mr Chumps, my tyrannosaurus rex.

'You think I'm well scary don't you, Mr Chumps?' I said, and I could hear the touch of desperation in my voice.

Mr Chumps didn't reply.

If Grandad was right and the real business of vampires was scaring, I'd have no right to call myself a proper vampire if I couldn't scare Gory at next full moon. I'd have no right to be a member of the Fang Gang. And I wanted to be a member of the Fang Gang even more than I wanted to be a member of the school football team. It was where I *belonged*.

And so it was with a heavy heart that, as the night drew in, I set out again towards the graveyard and the Fang Gang's headquarters.

Mr Cheng and the rest of the gang were already there. I could tell by the glum look on Mr Cheng's face that they had told him his head had gone missing.

'We even looked in the lost-property cupboard,' Griselda was saying.

'But we couldn't find it anywhere,' Scarlet went on. She smiled, a bit nervously, I thought. 'So we made you a new one.'

'Da-*daah*!' announced Griselda, dramatically, pulling the false head out of the black sack with a grand gesture.

There was a moment's silence. Then another. I think it was probably a good thing that Mr Cheng didn't have his head on his shoulders, that way we couldn't see the expression on his face.

We could only guess. And my guess was that it was a mixture of horror and pain.

'Try it on, then!' encouraged Griselda.

Slowly, Mr Cheng slipped the false head down on to his shoulders.

'What do you think?' asked Griselda, excitedly.

'Ah . . . er . . .' mumbled Mr Cheng. He was lost for words and no wonder. Now that the paint and glue had dried, the head looked even more like a kind of punk pineapple.

'Cool,' said Crombie.

'I'm sure no one will notice the difference,' chipped in Gory, quick to add insult to injury.

'Now you've got a false head, you'll be able to look for your proper one,' explained Griselda. 'It must be at school somewhere.'

'Yes, thank you. You have all been most er . . . *creative*,' said Mr Cheng, trembling. He lurched towards the door and stepped out into the frosty night.

'See you Monday!' chorused Scarlet and Griselda.

Mr Cheng didn't reply, though I fancy I heard a deep groan come from deep within him somewhere.

Chapter 10

MONDAY MORNING I got a postcard from Gran.

HM Prison Grimpenmire
Dear Jonathan, Hope life in Goolish is treating you well. Last week I escaped from HM Prison Crooksville! I snuck out in a laundry basket. However, when I got out at the other end I found I was in HM Prison Grimpenmire, the laundry van's next stop. Do you or your grandad Leech have any useful tools, e.g. angle grinder, pneumatic drill, JCB, which you could send me? Your affectionate gran xxxx

Jonathan Leech
Drac's Cottage
Goolish

I was still thinking about prisons and criminals as I walked through the school gates with Scarlet and saw that the playground was full of police cars.

'What's going on?' I asked Scarlet.

'I don't know,' she replied, 'but I've got a good idea.'

As soon as we got into the cloakrooms, Ms Blossom, our head teacher (as opposed to Mr Cheng, who was our head*less* teacher), ushered us all into the school hall.

Then, when everyone had settled down, Ms Blossom, flanked on either side by a burly police officer, got up on to the stage.

'Children,' she announced. 'Over the weekend a dreadful thing has happened. Our school has been broken into and the art room totally wrecked.'

There were gasps all around, including from Crombie, who hadn't quite twigged what this was all about.

'Sergeant Holmes and PC Watson from Goolish Police Station are in school this morning, searching for clues.'

By the time we got back to our classroom, the whole place was buzzing with excitement. Gory was under the sink with his magnifying glass and the rest of the class were on their hands and knees looking for fingerprints – or it might have been footprints. *Mr Cheng won't stand a chance with this lot*, I thought.

Then the door swung open and in strode Mr Cheng. He had his false head on and a Man U scarf round his neck to cover up the join.

'Sit down, everyone!' ordered Mr Cheng.

Everyone took one look at Mr Cheng and sat down.

Mr Cheng strode over to Gory's desk and put out his hand. 'Magnifying glass, please, Gory,' said Mr Cheng. Gory handed over his magnifying glass without a word. 'You can collect it from me at the end of school,' said Mr Cheng.

It was Tiffany – who else – who put up her hand. 'Are you all right, sir? Only you look a bit er . . . sort of . . . *odd*.'

'You mean the bright red scar under my ear?' asked Mr Cheng.

Tiffany nodded.

'And the black and blue bruising on my left cheek?'

Tiffany nodded again.

'I found myself in a spot of bother with a gang of thugs at the weekend,' explained Mr Cheng. 'I'm happy to say they came off worse.'

The class all gasped.

'And the purple eyebrows?' asked Tiffany.

'Merely the iodine that the paramedics put on my wounds,' said Mr Cheng, quickly. 'Now, everyone get out their English draft books, please.'

As the day wore on Mr Cheng grew more and more relaxed and in the afternoon he even told us all a couple of jokes.

I told Scarlet about Tiffany's stakes and the fact that she had called a Stake and Garlic Club meeting for after school.

'Just make sure you find out as much as you can about her vampire slaying plans,' she said, 'and report to the Fang Gang headquarters at dusk. Mr Cheng has asked to meet us.'

We had another football practice for the Inter-Schools' Cup match. I scored a hat trick. Gory was substituted. He looked absolutely livid.

Chapter 11

As soon as I got to Tiffany's, she took me out into her garden. There, laid out on the ground, were twelve stakes, a rubber mallet and one of those life-size blow-up Santas that people stick on the front of their houses at Christmas.

'Now, for a practice,' said Tiffany. 'I'll hold one of the stakes over Father Christmas' heart and you bang it in with the rubber mallet.'

She picked up a stake and held it over Father Christmas' heart. Unfortunately, the stake was

long and I am short. Even when I stretched, there was no way I could reach the top of the stake.

'Need the stepladders,' Tiffany said. Off she went, leaving me holding the stake.

Tiffany came back with a pair of step-ladders.

'Up you go!' she ordered.

I climbed the stepladders and gave the top of the stake an enormous wallop. There was a burp and a hiss from the inflatable Father Christmas and then he expired.

'Brilliant,' said Tiffany, getting down from the stepladders. 'I can get us some garlic off Mum and then we'll be ready.'

'The garlic thing's always puzzled me,' I said with a frown. 'I don't understand why vampires hate it so much. I know it stinks a bit, but not half as much as Brussels sprouts do.'

'You're right there,' agreed Tiffany. 'Sprouts would do the job much better.' She thought for a moment. 'Only one thing though.'

'What?'

'We'll have to rename the club the Stake and Brussels Sprouts Club.'

'Fine by me,' I said, feeling rather pleased with myself for leading Tiffany off the scent. Then she dropped her bombshell.

'My nan's knitting us a couple of black balaclavas,' she said. 'So that when we go to the graveyard we can merge into the darkness like proper vampire slayers.'

I gulped. 'The graveyard?' Tiffany knew where the Fang Gang hung out!

'Of course the graveyard!' said Tiffany. 'Where else do you think we'll find vampires? Sitting in the burger bar having a big brunch and extra fries? No, the graveyard is where they'll be. And the graveyard is where we'll be also.'

I was fed up and angry as I made my way to the Fang Gang's headquarters at dusk. Vampires, werewolves and ghouls had to be the most stupid sort of people ever. Anyone else would have had the brains to find a really good secret hideout to do their stuff, but vampires, werewolves and ghouls just *had* to use the graveyard every full moon. Even a vampire slayer as gormless as Tiffany had no trouble working out when and where to find them.

It wasn't just that I was worried that one of Tiffany's garden stakes might end up being hammered through Grandad's heart – or even my heart – I also knew that once Tiffany had spotted Grandad, the Moons, Mort and the Fang Gang up to their tricks, she would snitch on us to her mother. Mrs Bliss, being an investigative journalist, would investigate. Then she would appear on TV, demanding that all vampires, werewolves and ghouls be driven out of Goolish. Our lives would become unbearable.

When I got to the hut I told the gang about the stake, the inflatable Father Christmas and the Brussels sprouts and they all thought it a huge joke. Apart from Gory, that is, who just kept glowering at me.

When Mr Cheng appeared we gave him a huge round of applause.

'That false head gave me the sort of confidence I never knew I had,' he said. 'It was my most enjoyable day of teaching. Thank you all very much.'

'We could make you another if you like,' said Scarlet, enthusiastically.

'Actually, it's not another false head that I need, so much as my own one back. You see, telling the rest of the teachers and your class that I'd been in a fight is one thing. But parents' evening is coming up.'

'Yes, it's on the evening of the next full moon,' said Gory, shooting me an evil look.

'That's right,' said Mr Cheng. 'I'm sure some of the parents will twig that something's not quite right with my head. But even if I get through parents' evening all right, there is still the question of Ayesha.'

'Who's Ayesha?' asked Scarlet.

'My girlfriend,' said Mr Cheng. 'She's a zombie and although I'm sure she'll agree with me that it's a very nice papier mâché head you have made me, I rather think she'd prefer my proper one.'

'Don't you have any idea where your head might be?' I asked Mr Cheng.

'Well, I'm pretty sure nothing terrible has happened to it, like it being thrown out with the rubbish and crushed into dust up at the council tip,' said Mr Cheng. 'I'd soon know if something like that had happened to it. I'd *feel* it.'

We all shivered.

'No, I get the feeling that it's shut up somewhere in a small, dark space.'

'Perhaps you'll just have to wait until the hair on your head has grown really, really long,' said Scarlet, 'then it'll spread all over and we'll see a strand of it somewhere and follow it back till we reach your head.'

'Scarlet!' snapped Gory, 'you're talking like a twit.'

'Sorry,' said Scarlet, blushing.

I glowered at Gory. 'She was only trying to help,' I said. 'No need to take that attitude. Have you got a better idea?'

Gory glowered back at me. 'You,' he said, jabbing a finger at me, 'need to watch your step. I don't trust you and that Tiffany.'

'Boys, boys!' said Mr Cheng, sharply.

'I suppose the only thing we can do, then,' said Griselda, 'is to keep looking.'

Chapter 12

I GOT HOME TO FIND a bowl of Grandad's shirts in the kitchen sink. Grandad was leaning against the draining board, studying a book called *One Hundred and Thirteen Ways to Remove Ghastly Bloodstains*.

'OK, Grandad,' I said, sitting down at the table. 'What's with washing your shirts?'

'Shirts have to be washed,' said Grandad, airily.

'Yes, but yours never have been, have they?'

'A vampire's got to look smart if he's going to meet the most beautiful woman in the world,' said Grandad.

'Ah, so you're meeting her tonight at the graveyard, are you?' I asked him.

'Not at the graveyard,' said Grandad.

'Then where?' I asked.

Grandad's eyes drifted to the notice board that hung on the side of the Welsh dresser. Pinned to it was a copy of the school newsletter advertising the parents' evening. In the top left-hand corner of the newsletter was a photo of our head teacher, Ms Blossom.

'Isn't she a fine-looking woman?' said Grandad, with a sigh.

I couldn't see it myself, but then I suppose I wasn't a proper vampire. Yet. If Grandad's words had had the effect of turning my legs to jelly, his next words had the effect of turning my knees to blancmange.

'As soon as she hears me singing one of my songs she won't be able to resist me –'

'No, Grandad!'

'All that practice with the karaoke machine will have paid off!'

'No, Grandad!'

'I've always had the reputation of being something of a ladies' man –'

'No, Grandad,' I shouted. 'You are not to sing your love song to Ms Blossom!'

Grandad appeared not to hear me. 'Oh, that long, slender neck,' he murmured, with a sigh.

'Grandad, if you can't control yourself at parents' evening, you're not coming,' I said. 'You're not my parent, after all.'

'I'm responsible for your education while your parents are away. I don't suppose I'll be the only grandparent there, you know.'

'Watch my lips, Grandad,' I said firmly. 'I mean I don't want you there, understand?'

'I see,' said Grandad, with a hurt look. 'Ashamed of your old grandad, are you?'

'I will be, if you start singing stuff like "by heck, you've got a lovely neck" to Ms Blossom,' I replied. 'And it's the night of the full moon –'

'Yes, lucky that,' said Grandad.

'It's not lucky at all!' I shouted.

'I don't see the problem,' said Grandad. 'What woman in her right mind wouldn't thrill at being serenaded by an admirer?'

'A young, hunky, handsome admirer, maybe,' I said. 'A scrawny old vampire, no.'

'I see,' said Grandad, quietly. 'I see. I'm sorry I'm such a disappointment and an embarrassment to you, boy. Just when we seemed to be getting on so well.'

Grandad shuffled away, out through the kitchen. I heard his slow tread on the stairs and ran out to the hall.

'Grandad!' I called.

But it was too late. There was no answer, just a firm click as he shut his bedroom door.

Chapter 13

THE NIGHT OF THE FULL moon grew steadily closer. Tiffany was busy sharpening her garden stakes and buying up every available Brussels sprout in Goolish.

I was trying to keep away from Drac's Cottage as much as possible; the more Grandad practised with the karaoke machine, the worse his singing seemed to get. Besides, we were hardly speaking to each other.

Gory, Griselda, Scarlet and I made regular attempts to try and find Mr Cheng's head but we had no luck. Besides which, Gory and I were being kept pretty busy with football practice. Mr Hacker thought Gory might make twelfth man, which didn't please him hugely.

One morning, a very strange letter arrived for me. It was all made up of different letters cut from newspapers and magazines, just like you read about in detective stories. That evening, I took it up to the woods behind Drac's Cottage to have a good look at it. I thought it might be a message from Gran.

B*i*g **w**h**I**r**l**Y *b***I**rd
FLies n**E***s***t** s**o**o**n!**

I couldn't make head nor tail of it, but as I sat there in the gathering dusk, a strange sound caught my ear. A low, gentle howling. For just the briefest of moments it filled me with alarm, then I began to be strangely captivated – even entranced by it.

I crept through the woods towards the direction of the howling. I came to a small clearing and there, sitting with her back to a large pine tree, gazing up at the misty moon, was Scarlet.

She hadn't heard me and carried on howling. Then, I must have stood on a twig or

something, because she stopped suddenly and turned around with a frightened look.

'Oh, hi, Scarlet,' I said. 'What are you doing up here?'

'I often come up here to practise my howling,' said Scarlet. 'Trying to make it scarier. I couldn't bear the thought of growing up and not being able to behave like a proper werewolf.'

I went and sat down next to her in the clearing.

'Of course you'll grow up into a proper werewolf,' I said. 'I mean, your aunt and uncle are werewolves, your dad was a werewolf . . .'

'Yes, but my mum isn't,' said Scarlet. 'I think that's why she left Goolish.'

'But all the signs are there, your hands . . . and your howling is really very good. I don't ever think of you as anything else but a werewolf.'

Scarlet smiled, thoughtfully. 'So what have you been up to?'

'Oh, thinking and stuff,' I said with a shrug.

'What stuff?'

'Oh, you know,' I said.

'Actually, I don't,' said Scarlet. 'Otherwise I wouldn't have bothered to have asked, would I?'

Like most girls, Scarlet was dead nosy. But as werewolf girls go, she was OK. So I told her about the strange letter.

'"Big Whirly Bird Flies Nest Soon"? It doesn't make any sense,' Scarlet said, frowning. 'Who do you think it's from?'

'Gory,' I said. 'He's got it in for me. He might lose his place in the football team because of me. Though what his message means exactly, I've no idea. Perhaps it's a ghoulish curse or something.'

Scarlet sighed. 'He's so stupid at times. A real big ghoul's blouse.'

I laughed. Then I told her all about Grandad and how he fancied Ms Blossom and it was Scarlet's turn to laugh.

'I don't see what's funny about it,' I protested.

'He was the same last year with the woman from the fish and chip shop,' said Scarlet. 'One evening of the full moon he went in the shop, leaned right over the counter and bent down over her, intending to bite her neck.'

'What happened?'

'She slapped him round the face with a large battered cod,' said Scarlet, with another laugh, 'and your grandad's not eaten fish and chips since. But you can't stop him going to the parents' evening if he wants to. Don't worry about it. You'll be there to make sure he doesn't disgrace himself. And anyway, Ms Blossom can handle herself all right.'

I shrugged. I wasn't convinced.

'Parents' evening promises to be the night to end all nights,' I said with a sigh. 'Mr Cheng will be exposed, unless somehow he's got his head back by then. Grandad will be making a fool of himself with Ms Blossom. Tiffany will be snooping around the graveyard, looking for me to hold her stakes and Brussels sprouts for her, and I'll be giving Gory a good laugh by not being able to do any serious scaring.'

'I don't know what you're moaning about *that* for. You voted yourself to do it,' said Scarlet, unsympathetically.

'What else could I do? You and your howling, Gory and his ghostly shimmering, Griselda and her ability to turn into a bat at will; everyone's got scary dark-side gifts, except me. All I've got is a bit of strength and a turn of speed. Like Grandad said, scaring's the real mark of a vampire. And I'm just not scary. I'll tell you what, if I could find a way of

getting out of Goolish by next full moon, I'd take it.'

'Don't be so negative,' said Scarlet.

'What do you expect me to do,' I replied. 'Jump up and down with excitement saying "Oh, full moon, I can't wait!"?'

'Something will turn up,' said Scarlet.

'You think so?' I said, doubtfully.

'Of course,' answered Scarlet. 'Us were-wolves are brought up to believe that, if nothing else. It's the way we are. There have been many times during their history when wolves have found it hard to find food and warmth or shelter. But they always believed they would survive, and they did.'

The mist had cleared now and Scarlet and I leaned back against the pine trees and stared at the moon for a long time. Clouds floated behind it, so that it looked like an out-of-shape balloon, drifting slowly across the night sky.

'So far away, but so, so powerful,' said Scarlet. 'If you're really from the dark side, Jonathan, and I just *know* you are, you must believe in the moon.'

'Huh,' I said, gloomily.

Scarlet got up and dusted herself down. 'There's another week to go before the night of the full moon,' she said. 'Plenty of time for us to find Mr Cheng's head and for you to practise your power runs down the wing so that Goolish can beat Lady Daphne Freebody's in the Cup.'

Somewhere in the back of my mind I felt there was a connection between those two things but, try as I might, I couldn't work out what it was.

Chapter 14

THE CUP MATCH against Lady Daffy's – which was what everybody in Goolish called Lady Daphne Freebody's – was taking place on Wednesday after lunch, and the whole of Goolish School had the afternoon off to stand on the touchline and watch.

Lady Daffy's thought they were a pretty classy bunch and to prove it wore purple jumpers and yellow-and-green striped ties.

From what the others said there was a fair bit of history between them and Goolish and the casualty department at the local hospital had been put on full alert.

I was glad to see that Mr Hacker had decided to play Gory, after all. 'No fancy stuff, Leech. Keep it simple,' Gory hissed to me, as we ran out on to the pitch.

All the old footballs we had been practising with had been put away. A good thing too, for most of them were battered and flat and at least one of them had indelible ink drawings on it of Ms Blossom.

Mr Hacker had been keeping a set of new footballs in a string net in the boot of his car. He placed one of these new footballs on the centre spot ready for kick-off. He was going to be refereeing. Mr Cheng and the Lady Daffy's PE teacher were running the touchlines.

We all stood there waiting for Mr Hacker to blow his whistle for kick-off. I focused my eyes on the ball.

And then I noticed the ball focusing *its* eyes on me.

Suddenly, everything slotted into place in my brain. Mr Cheng leaving his head on the staffroom table, where the teachers always left their stuff. Mr Cheng's comments about him feeling his head was in a small and dark place. The link I'd felt there must be between Scarlet's comments about looking for Mr Cheng's head and the football match. Mr Hacker must have picked up Mr Cheng's head with the new footballs he'd bought for the match. All this time, Mr Cheng's head had been nestling in the net football bag in the boot of Mr Hacker's car! It wasn't a new football waiting to be booted up the field by the captain of Lady Daffy's School football team; it was Mr Cheng's head!

Mr Hacker blew his whistle and the Lady Daffy's captain lunged forward. With a surge of energy, I dived forward, rugby style, scooped up Mr Cheng's head and rolled out of the way of Lady Daffy's captain's boot. I was just in time to see him kick clean air and land painfully on his bottom, before I was on my feet again and preparing to run for it.

Mr Hacker was blowing his whistle so hard his cheeks stuck out like a hamster's. On the near touchline Lady Daffy's PE teacher appeared to be doing an impression of King Kong. On the far touchline I could just see Mr Cheng standing there, frozen to the spot.

There were eleven Lady Daffy players between me and him and all of them – with the exception of Lady Daffy's captain, who was still sitting on the ground – were charging my way. By now, Mr Cheng had worked out just what it was I was holding under my arm and he too started running towards me.

My first concern was to get the ball away from the Lady Daffy lot, so I turned and ran. Too late, as I pushed off for a power run, I realised that there was something on the ground blocking my path: Lady Daffy's captain, still rubbing his bottom.

'Jonathan, to me!' screamed a voice on my left, as I felt myself going over. There was Scarlet, standing on the touchline, waiting for the pass. I threw Mr Cheng's head to her and she caught it cleanly.

Immediately, Mr Hacker charged towards Scarlet. He wanted his new ball back and Scarlet was going to have her work cut out trying to see him off.

But I was up on my feet in no time and

quickly surging through the massed purple shirts of Lady Daffy's team.

'Back to me, Scarlet!' I yelled.

Scarlet's was not the straightest of throws, but I managed to juggle Mr Cheng's head with one hand, while giving Lady Daffy's goalkeeper a shove with the other. I turned on my heels again and surged forward. The rest of the field was clear before me and I powered on, leaping over the fence behind the goal-posts and straight on to the footpath that went all the way along the side of the school.

I didn't stop until I reached the little swing gate at the end of the footpath. Only then did I dare to turn round. I needn't have worried, I'd left the Lady Daffy lot far behind. But coming up fast towards me was Mr Cheng himself. I'd never seen such a turn of speed from a teacher.

I stepped off the path and ducked behind one of the tumbledown allotment sheds that ran behind the school. In a couple of seconds, Mr Cheng had joined me.

'That was some run, Jonathan,' he said. 'Thank you, you've saved my life.'

'I don't know about that,' I replied, 'but I have saved your head.'

I held out his head for him and he took off his papier mâché one and replaced it with his own.

'Ah, that is just so much better,' he said.

'Are you going back to the match?' I asked.

'You must be joking!' said Mr Cheng in alarm. 'No, the first thing I've got to do now is to dash home and wash my hair. There's mud all over it! I'll catch you later, Jonathan, thank you!'

I watched Mr Cheng race away across the allotments. Once he was out of sight, I bent down and picked up his papier mâché head. It was a bit battered in places and the cleaners' mop on top needed a good brush, but all in all I thought it had worn rather well.

I was feeling pretty pleased with myself when . . .

'Jonathan?' a voice whispered behind me.

Chapter 15

I SPUN ROUND AND found myself face to face with Tiffany. She looked down at Mr Cheng's papier mâché head in my hands and screamed.

There was no way I was going to hang around trying to explain to Little Miss Vampire Slayer just what I was doing round the back of the allotments, holding the head of her favourite teacher. I wasn't quite sure what to do with it, so I said the first thing that came into my head.

'Here, catch!' I yelled, throwing Mr Cheng's spare head to Tiffany.

'Eiaghhh!' she yelled. But she caught the head fair and square. Then with a look of sheer terror on her face she looked the head straight in the eye, screamed again and promptly fainted.

By now, Griselda, Scarlet, Crombie and Gory had joined me.

'What have you done?' asked Scarlet, with an appalled look.

'Er . . . she didn't seem to like the look of Mr Cheng's head,' I explained.

'She's not the only one,' commented Gory. 'It's a right mess.'

Gory was right. In her terrified state, Tiffany had held on to Mr Cheng's head so tightly that it was all battered and squashed.

Tiffany stirred a little and groaned.

'Hey, man,' said Crombie the Zombie, suddenly. 'You've just become a vampire slayer slayer. Cool!'

'What are you going to do?' asked Griselda, anxiously. 'You can't just leave her there.'

‘What do you expect me to do, give her the kiss of life?’ I replied, quickly.

‘If she comes round and sees that head in her hands she’ll only scream and faint again,’ Gory pointed out. ‘Then she’ll come round the third time, scream, faint, come round for the fourth time . . . it could go on for ever.’

‘Best get rid of it, then, hadn’t we?’ said Scarlet. She bent down and with her silky werewolf’s hands gently prised Mr Cheng’s tatty old head from Tiffany’s frantic grip. Then she threw it to Gory, who shimmered through

the wall of the nearest shed, then shimmered out again, empty-handed.

'I placed it over an upturned flower pot,' announced Gory. 'It's really going to give some old duffer a bit of a shock when he next turns up to do a spot of watering.'

'We'd best leg it back to the football field,' said Griselda.

'What? And leave me all alone with her?' I said, nodding in Tiffany's direction.

'It wouldn't look good if she came round to find the entire Fang Gang looming over her, would it,' Scarlet pointed out.

'But . . . what do I say to her?' I stammered in alarm. Gory and Crombie were already making their way back up the path.

'Don't worry, I'm sure you'll think of something,' said Griselda.

I shot a pleading look to Scarlet. But she just shrugged, as if to say, 'Griselda's right, this one has to be down to you and you alone, Jonathan.'

No sooner had Gory, Griselda, Crombie and

Scarlet scarpered back towards the playing fields than Tiffany opened her eyes. She stared, petrified, at her hands.

'But . . . what . . . where . . . ?' she stammered, her teeth chattering.

'But what where what?' I asked, gently.

'Mr Cheng's head . . . ?' she murmured. 'Where is Mr Cheng's head?'

'Mr Cheng's head?' I enquired, with a suitably puzzled look. 'Why, on his shoulders, I expect. That's where one usually finds heads. Isn't it?'

'But no . . . I remember now,' said Tiffany, suddenly. '*You* threw it to me!'

'I did *what*?' I asked, giving Tiffany my best amazed look. 'I think you must have had some sort of dream after you fainted.'

'I have not had some sort of dream!' said Tiffany, crossly. She frowned. 'You ran off the football pitch with the ball. Then Mr Cheng ran after you.' She looked around. 'Where is Mr Cheng?'

'Ah . . . Er . . .' I could sense that Tiffany's

questions were only going to get more and more difficult.

'And where is the ball?'

'Oh, I expect Mr Cheng's got it,' I said. 'Now, if you've fully recovered, shall we be getting back to the football pitch?'

'I don't like it,' muttered Tiffany, gloomily. 'There was *something* . . . I remember . . . "here, catch!" somebody said . . . yes, it's all slowly coming back to me . . .'

No one was keener than me to get away from Little Miss Vampire Slayer, but the further I got away from her, the closer I was getting to Mr Hacker, Ms Blossom and Lady Daffy's PE teacher, who were all standing in the middle of the pitch shouting at each other.

'It's a disgrace! An outrage!' the Lady Daffy teacher was yelling. He had one of those high, sarcastic voices that are better suited to old crows.

When he saw me approaching, he stopped screeching. Mr Hacker and Ms Blossom saw me too. None of them looked very happy and I could see that I wasn't exactly in the running for the Man of the Match Award.

Chapter 16

MR HACKER WAS SO angry he was lost for words. Ms Blossom was angry too, but being a head teacher, she *wasn't* lost for words.

'Where is the ball? And where is Mr Cheng?' she demanded to know, her face red with anger. Her neck was red too, and I could see what Grandad meant – it was very long and slender.

Now, my mum had taught me that the proper thing to do was to always tell the truth. But something told me that if I said, 'Mr Cheng? Oh, he's just nipped off home to wash his hair, Miss.' I'd be doing nobody any favours.

I was just trying to think up a suitable lie when Tiffany sidled up, her face as white as a sheet.

'Mr Cheng's been murdered!' she announced. 'And *he* –' Here she jabbed a finger at my chest, 'did it! He even threw me poor Mr Cheng's head . . . !'

And with that, her knees crumbled beneath her and she fainted again.

'Miss Goonhilly!' yelled Ms Blossom.

Miss Goonhilly came running up to Tiffany with her first-aid kit. Unfortunately, all she seemed to have in it was a small box of sticking plasters and a packet of cough sweets.

I stared at the ground, hoping against hope that a big hole would open up and swallow me. My head seemed to be filled with a loud, rushing noise. For a moment, I thought that perhaps I was going to go the way of Tiffany and crumple up on the ground in a dead faint.

Quickly I looked up to stop myself feeling dizzy. Then I saw everybody else was looking up too. And no wonder. For out of the sky a large yellow helicopter was dropping towards the ground and heading for the penalty spot. As it got closer, the wind from the blades made everybody's hair stand on end and we all took a few paces back.

Lady Daffy's team ran for their lives. Or rather, to be precise, they ran for their minibus. Their teacher started the engine and, with an impressive skid, slewed the vehicle round and headed off out of the school grounds, crashing into the far goalpost on the way.

The helicopter touched down, the pilot shut off the engines, the door flew open and a soldier in fatigues leapt out. He was holding a megaphone, which he raised to his mouth.

'I'm warning you. Everybody stay where you are!' he ordered. 'And let the boy go!'

Nobody moved. Except Tiffany, who had come round, but looked likely to faint yet again. Gory had been right. Unless somebody sorted her out once and for all, the fainting, coming round and fainting cycle could go on for ever.

A couple of other guys in fatigues emerged from the helicopter. I gasped when I saw one of them was holding what appeared to be a rifle. Then I looked again and saw that, in fact, it was a walking stick.

'This is your last warning,' said the man with

the megaphone, severely, scanning the faces of all the staff and pupils of Goolish School. Which I thought was a bit steep, as it was only the second warning we'd had. 'Let the boy go and no harm will come to anyone.'

Then suddenly, he lowered the megaphone and looked straight at me. 'Come along, Jonathan,' he said. 'Your ordeal is over now. *The Big Whirly Bird Has Flown The Nest.*'

It all came back to me in a rush: Dad's post-card about the retired SAS officer. The strange letter about the 'big whirly bird'. Of course, how else would a retired SAS officer attempt a rescue mission, except in a helicopter? And how had I been so stupid not to work that out, but to think the note had come from Gory?

The disappearance of Mr Cheng, the ruin of the football match, Grandad and parents' evening, Tiffany's stakes and Brussels sprouts, Gory, the need to somehow do some serious scaring . . . the night of the full moon . . . the whole vampire thing . . . I didn't have to deal with any of it any more! I could escape at last!

I ran forward towards the helicopter.

Chapter 17

WHEN I GOT CLOSE up to the guy with the megaphone, I saw that he was much older than he'd appeared from a distance. Almost as old as Grandad, in fact.

'Jonathan?' he barked, shaking me tightly by the hand. 'Captain Andy McNutty, SAS Retired. Now let's hop up into the old chopper and get out of here pronto back to friendly territory.'

As Captain McNutty led me to the helicopter door I turned back for one last look at Goolish School. I picked out the Fang Gang. Griselda, Gory and Scarlet stood there open-mouthed. Little Alfie was standing there with the infants, yelling, 'I want Jonathan! I want Jonathan!' Only Crombie looked as if the whole thing was beginning to bore him a little, but then what could you expect from a zombie?

Tiffany was on the ground still, though whether she'd fainted (again) or come round (again) I couldn't tell.

'Jonathan? Hurry along there!' called Captain McNutty. 'And where exactly is it you want to go?'

Where indeed? To Her Majesty's Prison Grimpenmire, to see Gran? To the SS *Albatross* in the South Atlantic to join Mum, Dad and their penguins? Where did I want to go? Despite standing accused of the murder of Mr Cheng, despite having a sworn enemy in Gory, despite being half the Stake and Garlic

Club, despite having a lovesick grandad, I wanted to be here, in Goolish. I felt I wanted . . . I felt I *needed* to be here for the next full moon. I belonged in Goolish. I was, after all, as Scarlet had pointed out, part of the dark side. More than that, like her, I knew I believed in the moon.

I turned to Captain McNutty. 'Actually, if it's all the same with you, I'd prefer *not* to be rescued, thank you very much. I want to stay here.'

'Well, we can't force you to come with us,' said Captain McNutty, with a shrug, 'but if the lads and I haven't got to swoop off right away, do you know if there's anywhere around here we can get a cup of tea?'

'The teachers are always drinking it in the staffroom,' I said.

'Excellent!' said Captain McNutty. 'Come on, you guys! Lead on, Jonathan!'

'If you don't mind, I'd prefer it if you led and I followed,' I said. 'Only Ms Blossom, the head teacher, is a bit cross with me because she thinks I've murdered Mr Cheng.'

'Are you sure you don't want us to whisk you away from this madhouse?' asked Captain McNutty.

'No,' I said, 'I'm sure.'

When we reached Ms Blossom, I said, 'Would it be possible for Captain McNutty and his men to have a cup of tea? Only they've had a long journey.'

'Miss Goonhilly!' called Ms Blossom. Miss Goonhilly was still with Tiffany, trying to decide whether to give her a sticking plaster or a cough sweet. 'I'm sure Tiffany's worked out how to recover from a faint by now. She seems to have had plenty of practice, anyway. Would you kindly go to the staffroom and put the kettle on, please.' Ms Blossom told Miss Goonhilly.

Miss Goonhilly trotted off.

'About Mr Cheng,' I began. 'I haven't murdered him, Miss, honest.'

'Of course you haven't, Jonathan,' said Ms Blossom. 'I can see you're not a murderer. You've got a far too angelic face for that.'

I wished people would stop saying that! I was a ruthless vampire, capable of doing some serious scaring! At least, I hoped I was.

Miss Goonhilly came running up, breathlessly.

'However,' Ms Blossom said to me, sternly, 'that still leaves the question: where is Mr Cheng?'

'In the staffroom,' said Miss Goonhilly. 'Making the tea. With a young lady named Ayesha. His girlfriend apparently, arrived for a visit.'

There was a thud behind me. I didn't bother to turn round. It was obviously Tiffany, fainting yet again. You couldn't blame her, really. First she'd found herself holding the decapitated head of her favourite teacher, then she'd learnt that all along he'd had a girlfriend called Ayesha. It just wasn't her day.

The whole school gathered in the hall. Mr Cheng appeared with Ayesha. She had a faraway look in her eyes, like zombies do. But apart from that she didn't look in the least like Crombie. Which was lucky for her and lucky for Mr Cheng too, I suppose.

Mr Cheng, of course, looked his old self again.

'I'm sorry I had to run off the football pitch like that,' he explained to Ms Blossom. 'Only the scars and the bruises on my face were giving me such gip I just had to go home and put some ointment on them. When I got there, I found Ayesha had turned up.'

'Well, you certainly look a whole lot better,' said Ms Blossom. 'Having Ayesha turn up unexpectedly like that seems to have made a new man of you.'

After they'd had their tea, Captain McNutty and his colleagues had their photos taken for the school newsletter. Then everybody went back to the field to watch them climb into their helicopter and swoop away over the hills and woods behind Goolish.

For a moment I panicked and thought I'd made a terrible decision. Perhaps I should have gone in the helicopter after all. It would have made things so much easier.

Then I heard a voice at my side say, 'Thank you, Jonathan.' I turned and saw Mr Cheng.

'Oh, that's all right,' I said, with a shrug. 'It was nothing, really.'

'On the contrary,' said Mr Cheng. 'It was quite something. That power run, especially. If there's ever anything I can do for you in return . . .'

I looked at Mr Cheng long and hard. 'You're a teacher, sir,' I said. 'Can you teach me to be seriously scary?'

Mr Cheng sighed. 'Come and see me after school tomorrow,' he said.

And so, the next day, as soon as everyone had gone home, I pulled a chair up to the side of Mr Cheng's desk.

'I understand how you feel, Jonathan,' said Mr Cheng. 'When I was your age I thought I'd never be given the gift of taking off my head. Each full moon I'd grab hold of it and pull it this way and that, but of course nothing ever happened. And then one night, when I was struggling trying to learn some spellings for a test the next day, I felt so weary I just lifted my head off my shoulders and put it on the desk in front of me for a rest. And since then, well, you know, of course . . .'

'So you're saying you can't teach me to be scary?' I said.

Mr Cheng nodded. 'When the time is right, your fangs will grow and you will be a terrible sight. Until then, you will just have to wait. Oh, and by the way, Tiffany's left a note on your desk.'

I went and picked the note up. It read:

Something wicked is going on and I know you've got something to do with it. Mr Cheng said it must have been some sort of laddish practical joke, but I don't believe him. You are herewith banned FOR LIFE!!! from the Stake and Brussels Sprouts club.

Tiffany

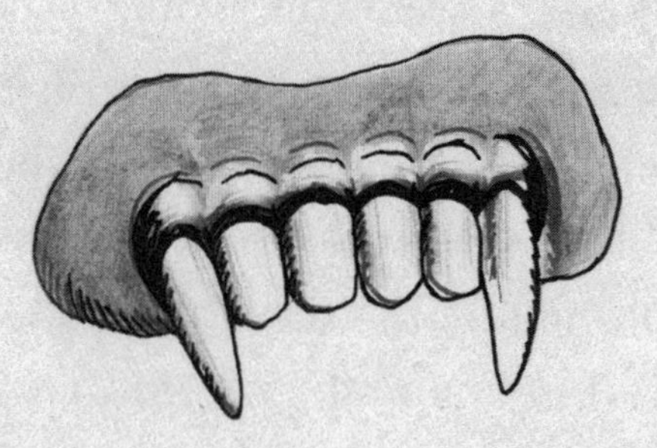

Chapter 18

THE DAYS TICKED BY towards parents' evening and the night of the full moon. I only had one conversation with Tiffany, but that was enough. She strode up to me in the playground one morning break, her eyes blazing with menace and determination.

'I thought you'd like to know that I told my mum what happened at the football match. She's going to come vampire slaying with me on the night of the full moon, so all the dreadful and disgusting things that go on will be reported in all the papers and on television.'

The thought crossed my mind that the first howl from a werewolf would send Tiffany into one of her faints. She must have known what I was thinking because she said:

'And I've been having Anti Fainting Therapy too, so it will take more than the sight of a toothy old vampire to scare me, so there.'

A couple of days after this encounter, I received a postcard from Dad:

SS *Albatross*, South Atlantic

Dear Jonathan
I've had a message from Captain McNutty who told me about your refusal to be rescued. I fear the worst. We will be coming back home early to rescue you ourselves. Just as soon as I can tear your mother away from the penguins.

Your loving dad

Jonathan Leech
c/o Mr Leech
Drac's Cottage
Goolish

At last, the day of the parents' evening and the night of the full moon eventually arrived. Early in the evening, I made my decision. I knew I was being weak and I'd probably live to regret it, but what the heck. I went down to the kitchen, where I found Grandad sitting gloomily at the table.

'Come on, Grandad,' I said. 'We don't want to be late for the parents' evening, do we?'

Grandad brightened. 'You've changed your mind?'

'There are two conditions,' I said. 'One: you don't sing your love songs, and two: you keep your fangs to yourself.'

I went back upstairs and wrote a list of things I had to do. It looked very daunting.

LIST OF THINGS TO DO

1: Make sure Grandad doesn't bite Ms Blossom.
2: Stop Tiffany and her mum slaying the Fang Gang.
3: Prove myself a real vampire by doing some serious scaring.
4: Finish maths homework.

As Grandad and I walked into the school I gave him a final word of warning:

'Remember, Grandad,' I said, sternly.

'I promise,' said Grandad. Though he had his hands behind his back and I just knew he had his fingers crossed.

'Ah, Jonathan and Mr Leech,' said Ms Blossom when we sat down at the desk in her office. 'Now, just let me find Jonathan's report . . .'

Ms Blossom bent down over her desk and like a shot Grandad bent down over her neck. His mouth was open and his fangs glistened in the bright fluorescent light.

Suddenly, without a blink, Ms Blossom sat up. 'Mr Leech, please, do try and control yourself,' she said in a voice she usually used when breaking up fights in the playground. 'I know it's a full moon, I always have my parents evenings on the night of the full moon. That way my vampire, werewolf, zombie and ghoul parents are more likely to come along, given that they're going to be out for most of the

night anyway. Take those false fangs out and put them back in your pocket – they are false fangs, I take it?'

'Yes . . .' mumbled Grandad.

'I thought so. Vampires your age don't usually still have their own.'

Grandad obediently took out his fangs.

'Now, I suggest you give them to Jonathan for safekeeping.'

Grandad obediently passed me his fangs and I put them in my pocket.

'Jonathan is a popular and very responsible member of our school community,' Ms Blossom said. And for one awful moment, I thought she was going to say I looked angelic too. But she didn't. 'You must be very proud of him, Mr Leech,' she added.

'I am,' said Grandad. 'I am. It's been such a treat having him staying with me.' He paused and coughed. 'There's just one other thing.'

'Oh?' enquired Ms Blossom.

'Yes, I've acquired this karaoke machine, you see –'

'Grandad!' I warned.

Grandad ignored me. 'The thing is,' he said, 'I haven't got much use for it . . .' He looked longingly at Ms Blossom's neck. 'Not now. So I wondered if you'd like it for the school. I know you've got a talent contest coming up.'

'Why, that's very generous of you, Mr Leech,' said Ms Blossom. 'Thank you very much.'

When we got outside the school, Grandad said, 'Well, I hope I didn't embarrass you, boy.'

'No,' I said. 'And, Grandad . . .'

'Yes, boy?'

'I quite like staying with you, too.'

'You do? That's good.' said Grandad. 'And, boy, about your scaring. I'll do what I can to help you, you know.'

It was kind of him to offer, I suppose, but I couldn't see what he could do now. It was all a bit too late for that.

'Now, I must rush off,' said Grandad. 'I've got things to do to get ready for the night. I expect you'll want to stay and chat with your friends?'

I nodded and watched Grandad stride off up the hill towards Drac's Cottage. I slipped my hands into my pockets and only then realised that I still had his false fangs. Without a second thought I took those fangs out of my pocket, and wiped them as clean as I could with my hanky. Then I slipped them into my mouth.

Now I was ready to do some serious scaring.

Chapter 19

SCARLET, GORY, GRISELDA, Crombie and I had agreed to meet at Scarlet's as soon as parents' evening finished so that we would be ready for anything that Tiffany and her mum might be planning. Scarlet's house was on the road up to the graveyard.

As I approached, I saw that the rest of them were already there. I ran up to them, holding my lips tightly on to Grandad's fangs. They all turned when they heard me coming and I waited for the screams of fear and terror. They didn't come. Instead, Griselda groaned.

'Jonathan? What are you doing?' she asked. 'Are those your grandad's fangs you've got shoved in your mouth?'

'Yesh,' I mumbled, not being able to say very much on account of my mouth being full of fangs.

Gory burst out laughing. 'This is what he thinks of as serious scaring, I suppose! Told you he wasn't really one of us!'

'Cool!' giggled Crombie.

'You've got till midnight,' threatened Gory. 'Then your days in the Fang Gang are over.'

'Oh, Jonathan,' sighed Scarlet. 'Take them out for goodness' sake and put them back in your pocket.'

As we walked up to the graveyard, Gory busied himself showing off. He shimmered in and out of cars, through hedges and lamp-posts. When we reached the graveyard, he even walked through half a dozen gravestones.

We reached the hut. It was locked.

'Open up, Gory,' said Griselda. 'We need to be able to get in here just in case we have to hide from Tiffany and her mum.'

Gory started to walk through the wall of the hut. Suddenly, he stopped and leapt back.

'Ow! My nose!' he moaned.

'Gory, what's the problem? Just walk through that wall and open up for us, would you?'

'I can't,' mumbled Gory, sadly.

'I don't believe it,' said Scarlet. 'He's used up all his shimmering powers mucking about on the way up here.'

'Shh!' said Crombie, urgently.

We listened. There was the sound of a car engine in the road below the graveyard. The engine stopped and a car door slammed.

'Tiffany and her mum!' whispered Scarlet.

'Wow, they *are* early,' said Griselda. 'Quick, everyone, hide!'

Immediately, there was a whoosh and

Griselda was gone. I just made out a bat form as she swooped up towards the safety of the church spire.

'No! You can't leave me!' cried Gory.

He was wrong. Scarlet's werewolf shape leapt over the fence and away, while the ground just seemed to swallow up Crombie the Zombie. Being on the small side, I dived behind the nearest gravestone. But Gory was tall and wide; for him there was no hiding place.

I peered out from behind my gravestone. Just a few metres away, down on the road, I could see Tiffany and her mum. They were wearing balaclavas and Tiffany was balancing a garden stake and a large bag of Brussels sprouts in her arms.

'It all seems very quiet to me, darling,' I heard Mrs Bliss say.

'No, shhh, there's somebody – or something – coming along the lane,' said Tiffany.

'Hello!' called a voice.

Striding up to Tiffany and her mum came Mr Cheng and Ayesha!

'Why, Tiffany! I almost didn't recognise you under that very smart balaclava. And you must be Mrs Bliss?' said Mr Cheng, cheerfully. 'I'm Mr Cheng and this is my girlfriend, Ayesha.'

'Cool!' said Ayesha.

'Mr Cheng?' said Mrs Bliss. 'Why, Tiffany's told me all about you. You're her favourite teacher! What are *you* doing up here?'

'Oh, you know, a romantic moonlight stroll and all that,' said Mr Cheng, with a swift glance towards the graveyard.

'We're vampire slaying,' said Tiffany.

'Vampires,' laughed Mr Cheng, nervously. 'Oh, I don't think you'll find any vampires up here –'

'Then what's that?' asked Tiffany, pointing up the path towards the hut.

Mr Cheng started. So did Ayesha. They and Mrs Bliss looked in the direction which Tiffany was pointing.

'That . . .' said Mr Cheng. 'Why, that isn't a vampire. That's a *Gory*.'

Gory wandered down towards Mr Cheng, Ayesha, Tiffany and her mum.

'Hello,' said Gory, sheepishly.

'Hello,' said Mr Cheng. 'Gory's not a vampire. And as you can see, he doesn't look the least bit scary. Mind you, he is rather pale . . .'

All this time, my head had been feeling a bit strange. I put my hand up to my face. Something was protruding from my mouth. Something long, sharp and smooth. Something that felt like . . . fangs.

I put my other hand to my mouth, and as I did so, Tiffany, who was still staring like mad, looking for creatures of the night, must have seen it, for she shouted:

'There! Behind that gravestone!'

Before anyone could stop her, she was bounding through the graveyard towards me, waving her stake like a giant javelin in one hand and her bag of Brussels sprouts in the other. It was now or never. As Tiffany came up to me, I popped my head up over the top of the gravestone.

'Aaaaargh!' screamed Tiffany, in terror. 'Aaargh!'

Mr Cheng had followed Tiffany and now he quickly pulled her away. 'It's all right, Tiffany,' he said. 'Just shadows in the dark.' And he led her off, sobbing, down to the road, but not before turning to give me a huge wink.

'She's obviously a very imaginative girl,' said Mr Cheng. 'Look, Mrs Bliss, why don't you and Tiffany come back with me and Ayesha for some supper? I don't really think we're likely to find any vampires tonight, do you?'

'No, you're right,' said Mrs Bliss. 'And I'm sure Tiffany would be thrilled to have supper with her favourite teacher.'

And they all climbed into Mrs Bliss's car. I ran down through the graveyard to the road, and just as Mrs Bliss was pulling away, gave Tiffany one last toothy look through the passenger window. Her screams echoed all the way down the hill.

I went back up to the graveyard and heard a howl behind me. I turned round and saw Scarlet in werewolf form, her coat shining in the moonlight and her tail waving like crazy. Next thing, a bat flew on to my head and whacked my ear. Then Crombie the Zombie rose from the ground and extended a muddy hand towards me.

'Cool!' he said.

I looked back towards the lane. Gory was standing there, staring at me. He came up to me and put a hand on my shoulder. 'I've got to admit it,' he said. 'That was some serious scaring. And those fangs of yours are well fearsome . . .'

Then I remembered something. 'Grandad's fangs!' I yelled. 'I've still got Grandad's fangs!'

'He'll know where to find them,' said Gory. And sure enough, a few moments later, Mort's hearse appeared with Grandad in the back.

'I don't think I really need these now,' I said, giving him back his fangs.

'No, boy,' said Grandad, with a gummy smile. 'I don't think you do. You look to me as if you're a proper young vampire now.'

Grandad wiped his fangs on his sleeve and popped them back into his mouth.

'You didn't forget them, did you, Grandad? You deliberately let me hold on to them hoping they'd help with my scaring.'

Grandad nodded.

Gradually, all the ghouls, zombies, werewolves and vampires of Goolish arrived at the graveyard. Grandad seemed to have got over his lack of success with Ms Blossom's neck and everyone partied long into the night. A little after midnight Mr Cheng and Ayesha turned up, having finally got rid of Mrs Bliss and Tiffany. Not long after that, I felt my mouth returning to its usual shape and I saw that Scarlet was now not so much werewolf as weregirl.

'Now,' she said to me, 'do you believe in the moon?'

'Yes,' I replied, 'and I guess that deep down, I always have.'

And we stood there, side by side, staring up at the sky, the full moon clear and bright above us.

Mr Cheng and Ayesha appeared.

'Quite a night, eh, Jonathan?' said Mr Cheng.

'Quite a night,' I agreed.

'I'm absolutely exhausted,' said Mr Cheng with a yawn. 'I think I'll just take my head off for a rest.'

'Actually, Mr Cheng,' I said, 'I think it might be better if you didn't.'

'Perhaps you're right, Jonathan,' said Mr Cheng, with a smile. 'Perhaps you're right.'